Dragon!

by

Hilary McKay

Illustrated by Mike Phillips

D0434427

You do not need to read this page – just get on with the book!

First published in 2006 in Great Britain by
Barrington Stoke Ltd
www.barringtonstoke.co.uk

Copyright @ 2006 Hilary McKay
Illustrations @ Mike Phillips

The moral right of the author has been asserted in
accordance with the Copyright, Designs and
Patents Act 1988

ISBN-10: 1-842994-17-4
ISBN-13: 978-1-84299-417-7

Printed in Great Britain by Bell & Bain Ltd

MEET THE AUTHOR – HILARY MCKAY

What is your favourite animal?
Fox
What is your favourite boy's name?
Jim
What is your favourite girl's name?
Bella
What is your favourite food?
Apples
What is your favourite music?
Classic rock and Bach
What is your favourite hobby?
Natural History

MEET THE ILLUSTRATOR – MIKE PHILLIPS

What is your favourite animal?
Dog
What is your favourite boy's name?
Ben (my son's name)
What is your favourite girl's name?
Hannah and Olivia (my daughters)
What is your favourite food?
Cheese
What is your favourite music?
Anything that makes my feet tap
What is your favourite hobby?
Armchair cricket supporting

To Dip,
with love

Contents

Chapter 1
Witches Towers

Max was ten years old. He lived with his Aunt Emma.

Aunt Emma was a witch. She had a pointed hat and black clothes. She had all the witchy things that witches have. She lived in a place called Witches Towers.

She was not like any other aunt in the world.

She was *definitely* a witch.

Max and Aunt Emma liked each other, but Witches Towers was not a very peaceful place. Max was very stubborn. Aunt Emma had a very witchy temper.

A lot of the trouble at Witches Towers was because of Max's bedroom.

Sometimes the mess in Max's bedroom was awful. If you just opened the door, the junk came tumbling down the stairs.

This made Aunt Emma very angry. It made her bang her broomstick on the floor and shout, "This is the worst yet! I shall put up with no more!"

Max gave a shrug to show that he'd heard all this before.

This made Aunt Emma even more cross. She ran her hands through her witchy silver hair until sparks fell out and flew across the floor.

"It's not that far to the edge of the world, where children aren't allowed!" she shouted. "I have plenty of friends who live around there! And one day I'll go and join them! Then what will you do?"

Then she would rush around and stamp on the sparks before they burnt anything. While she did this Max would pick up the worst of the mess and push it under his bed.

He didn't worry one bit.

He didn't believe that Aunt Emma really would go and live at the edge of the world. He knew that she always calmed down in the end.

When Max was ten years old he started school in the village across the fields. The village was called Sleepy Hollow.

In Sleepy Hollow no one believed in witches. Max found this out on his first day at school.

"Why didn't you come here years ago?" asked everyone. "Were you too scared?"

"No," said Max. Max didn't get scared. And he always told the truth. "I didn't need to come to school. My aunt taught me everything."

"Everything!" they said.

"Well," said Max. "Nearly everything. Reading and writing. A is for Abracadabra ..."

"WHAT!" shouted everyone.

"B for Black. C for Cat. D for Dragon's eggs ..."

Everyone started laughing.

"What about P for Pointy Hats!" shouted someone. "What is your aunt? Some kind of witch?"

"Of course she's a witch!" said Max.

They laughed even more and they made signs to each other to show that they thought Max was crazy. He could see that they didn't believe him at all.

"My Aunt lives in Witches Towers," he said. "Not that far from the edge of the world!"

They nearly fell over with laughing. And they said, "Oh yes! As if! Whatever! Like we're going to believe that! Not!"

And then they walked off.

All except one.

Timmy Green.

"I believe you," said Timmy Green. "I believe you, Max!"

From that moment Max and Timmy Green were friends.

Timmy Green did not have a mother or father. He lived in the Children's Home in the village.

Timmy and Max were not at all alike.

Max was tall. Timmy was small. Max was scared of almost nothing, but Timmy was scared of almost everything.

"I like books," Timmy told Max. "They tell you things it's useful to know."

"I know everything I need to know already," said Max. "I only came to school because my witchy aunt made me. She got in a huff just as we got to P for Porridge. She said I could find out the rest at school."

"You can!" said Timmy. "I can help! After P, it's Q. Q for Quiet."

"I like Noise," said Max.

"Then R," said Timmy. "R for Rabbits. There's a very good book about rabbits in the library ..."

"I already know everything about rabbits," said Max.

"S for School ..."

Max yawned.

"T for Timmy ..."

"I like T for Timmy," said Max. "I think we should stop there."

Timmy was quite happy to stop at T for Timmy. He said, "Tell me about Witches Towers."

Chapter 2
Max's Great Secret

So Max told Timmy about Witches Towers.

"It's over there across the fields," Max said, and pointed back across the fields. "It has lots of little pointed roofs and a huge wooden door. There's a big bell which hangs over the door and a rope to pull to make it ring."

"Is there a garden?"

"There's a toad garden," said Max. "My aunt likes toads. The garden is full of big, warty, juicy ones."

Timmy shuddered.

"The rooms are dark with wooden walls and spiders everywhere."

Timmy gulped. He didn't like spiders.

"There are empty attics," said Max, "and I think they're haunted. I never go up there."

"Nor would I," said Timmy with a tremble.

"And then there's the roof," said Max. "That's my favourite place. There's a little stair that goes round and round all the way up to it. It comes out onto a flat place in the middle with pointed roofs all around. I'll show you when you come and visit me."

"V ... v ... v ... visit you?"

"We can climb the roof and look down over the edge," Max went on.

Timmy shivered so much he had to sit down.

"And you can see my witchy Aunt when she has a huff," said Max. "When can you come? Today?"

"N ... n ... not today," said Timmy.

"Tomorrow?"

"No," said Timmy. "N ... n ... not tomorrow."

"Soon?"

"M ... m ... maybe."

"Good," said Max. "Then I'll show you my Great Secret that I found in the fields. I've been waiting to show someone for ages. I've got it hidden under my bed. Guess what it is! I'll give you a clue, it's gold!"

"Gold?"

"And it's warm."

"Warm?"

"It's a beauty! Very, very heavy and bigger than a football. But it's egg-shaped, of course!"

"Is it an egg?" asked Timmy.

"You guessed that fast!" Max said. "But what sort of egg? You'll never guess that in a million years! My aunt has always wanted one like this, that's why I've got to keep it such a secret! What's the matter?"

Timmy was staring at Max with his eyes wide open. He looked terrified.

Timmy had read every single book in the library. He had read all the Nature books twice. He knew which eggs were gold and heavy and bigger than a football.

He said, "It's a dra ... a dra ... a dragon's egg!"

"Yes," said Max proudly. "Clever old T for Timmy!"

"B ... b ... but dragons' eggs are very dangerous! I read it in a book ..."

"Pooh! Books!" said Max.

"That they go b ... b ... b ...!" Timmy tried to say.

"You can't believe books!" said Max. "They're not real life! Now, I know ALL about dragon's eggs! I've GOT a dragon's egg! I'm going to keep it until it hatches and then I'll have a baby dragon!"

"But what will you do with a baby dragon?" asked Timmy.

"I shall keep it on the roof," said Max proudly.

Timmy said, "You CAN'T keep a dragon on the roof!"

"Watch me!" said Max.

Chapter 3
Aunt Emma's Huff

Max and Timmy were best friends, but they had a few problems. Max would never listen to what Timmy's book said about the terrible danger of dragons' eggs. Timmy would never agree that it was a good idea for Max to keep a dragon on the roof.

"It will try to escape," said Timmy.

"I will tame it," said Max

"It will grow very big."

"The roof is huge."

"What about when it learns to fly?"

"It hasn't even hatched yet," said Max.

Timmy shivered at the thought of the dragon's egg-hatching. He tried again to get Max to read the dragon book.

"I'm much too busy right now," said Max. He wanted to make a new notice for his bedroom door. He had made a lot of them lately. They were meant to keep his Aunt out. That way, she wouldn't find the dragon's egg.

Max showed Timmy some of his notices, because he thought they were funny.

ROSES ARE RED, RABBITS HAVE FLUFF,
AUNTS HAVE TOADS
AND THEY GET IN A HUFF.

KNOCK AND KNOCK AND KNOCK
BUT DON'T COME IN!

MAX'S ROOM, PRIVATE PLACE, DO NOT DARE SHOW YOUR FACE.

The notices worked. They kept Aunt Emma out of Max's room. But they made her very cross. She banged the floor with her broomstick and pulled sparks out of her hair and said she would go to the edge of the world where no children were allowed.

Max loved it when she did these witchy things.

"You should see her!" he said to Timmy. "You should come! What about today?"

"Too much homework," said Timmy.

"Tomorrow?"

"P ... perhaps not tomorrow."

"Soon?"

"Oh yes! Soon!" agreed Timmy.

Then Max made his best notice ever.

NO FREAKY BROOMSTICK PEOPLE

When Aunt Emma saw it she was so cross that she pulled open Max's door to tell him what she thought of him.

Max had not tidied his room for ages. A wave of old clothes, footballs, dirty plates, muddy boots, and a hundred other things fell out of the door and rolled Aunt Emma right down the stairs and into the garden.

Then Aunt Emma had her biggest huff ever.

Sparks shot out of her hair like comets. She grabbed her broomstick and there was a white flash of fire.

"I'm off!" said Aunt Emma. "To stay with my friends at the edge of the world (no children allowed)! And I won't be back until you have tidied your bedroom!"

Then there was a bang and a roar like thunder and a lot of black smoke.

After that there was nothing.

No broomstick. No pointy hat. No Aunt Emma.

She had always said that one day she would go. Now she had done it.

Max stood in the garden. It smelled like fireworks.

The silence was awful.

Then from up in his bedroom came a little sound. A small clink like breaking china.

Perhaps it was because of the enormous bang. Perhaps it would have happened anyway.

The dragon's egg was finally hatching.

Chapter 4
All Alone

Max jumped over the pile of junk that had knocked Aunt Emma down the stairs, and ran up to his bedroom as fast as he could. He was sure a baby dragon would be waiting there.

But nothing had changed. He pulled the dragon's egg out from under his bed, and it was as gold and solid as ever.

Then suddenly Max saw something new. A dark line now zig-zagged across the golden shell.

Max's heart thumped. It thumped harder than when Aunt Emma had vanished on her broomstick. It thumped harder than on the scary day when he first started school.

"It's hatching at last!" Max whispered.

If he could have had one wish it would have been that Timmy could watch the egg hatching too.

Meanwhile, things were happening in the village. Everyone had noticed the flash of white light, the thick black smoke, and the rumble of the broomstick.

The streets were buzzing with excitement.

"A lightning strike!" people said. "A lightning strike has hit poor Miss Emma's house!"

In no time at all about a hundred people were running to the rescue. They took with them first aid boxes, sandwiches, blankets and cameras. They ordered the children to stay behind. Most of the children took no notice. They came too.

Everyone felt very good. They were excited by the smell of fireworks and smoke drifting across the fields. They were glad that they were not the ones struck by lightning.

But when they got to Witches Towers they were a bit sorry to see that it looked just the same as always.

No one came when they banged on the door.

Max was still in his bedroom. He heard the bangs, but he was not polite.

"I'm not answering!" he said crossly to himself. "I'm just not! The egg could hatch at any moment! Whoever's banging will have to go away."

But no one went away. Instead Max heard the sound of the front door being pushed open. Then footsteps and helpful voices on the stairs.

"Cooee! Anyone home, Miss Emma?"

"We thought we should pop over!"

"Max? Are you there, Max, dear?"

"Bother!" said Max.

He heard the footsteps stop at his bedroom door. He heard whispering. People were reading his notices. They sounded shocked.

"Bother, oh bother, oh BOTHER!" grumbled Max. But he opened his bedroom door, stepped outside and closed it quickly.

There was a huge crowd on the landing and on the stairs.

"There's loads of you!" said Max, and he stared at them all. "Did Timmy come?"

The crowd looked at each other, and then shook their heads.

"Pity," said Max. "Oh well. I'm afraid I'm terribly busy! So, goodbye."

No one took this big hint. They all began to talk at once.

"Thank goodness you're not hurt!"

"Such a storm, but over so quickly! Dreadful lightning!"

"What very rude notices on your bedroom door, Max!"

"Your poor dear Aunt! Where is she?"

"Gone," said Max. All he wanted was to get back to his dragon's egg.

"Gone?" asked someone in a soft voice.

"On her broomstick," Max said. "That was the bang you heard. I'm perfectly safe! It wasn't lightning at all!"

But no one was listening. They said, "Struck by lightning! How very sad! She must have been vaporised!"

"Vaporised?" asked Max.

"Frizzled into nothing, dear," said the lady from the Children's Home. "Well, you must come back with us, I suppose!" the lady went on. "We are very crowded, but after your sad loss …"

"You don't understand!" cut in Max. "She wasn't frizzled! There was no lightning! My Aunt just whizzed off on her broomstick. In a huff (as always). She always said she'd go one day. And I can't come to the Children's Home, I'm very busy here!"

It was just like the first day of school all over again.

No one believed him and no one listened. They said he was unkind. They said he wasn't funny. They said what a dreadful way to talk about his poor frizzled Aunt.

They wouldn't listen when Max said he'd be all right on his own.

"You'll be lonely, Max dear," they said.

"I LIKE being lonely!" said Max

"What if you need help? No one will know."

"I'll shout!" said Max.

"We'll never hear."

"I'll call out! I'll yell! I know what! I'll ring the bell!"

"What bell?" they asked.

"I'll show you!"

Max pushed past all the people, ran downstairs, pulled a table onto the front porch, lifted a chair onto the table, stood on the chair, climbed onto the box and pulled the long bell rope.

The noise of that bell made everyone jam their hands on their ears and beg Max to stop.

After a while he did.

"You'd hear that!" said Max, and they had to say that he was right.

Even so, it was a long time before they agreed that Max could stay at Witches Towers just for one more night. They made him say that he would ring the bell the moment he needed them, and they promised they would come running the moment they heard it.

After that they left the sandwiches they had brought. They put them in tidy heaps around the garden.

Then they went home at last.

Max had been worrying about his dragon egg all the time. He rushed back to it as soon as the crowd had gone away.

It was just as he had left it, warm and round, with a dark zig-zag line across the gold shell.

"Good," said Max, and he sat down on the floor by the egg. He tried to feel happy that he hadn't missed anything, and that his witchy aunt had gone, and that the village people had gone. Now he was free at last to do just as he liked.

"Perfect," said Max. "Nearly."

"Perfect, but a bit lonely," said Max, and he wished that Timmy was there.

Chapter 5
The Bell

The house was terribly quiet. There was no witchy singing anywhere downstairs. No rattle of witchy cooking from the kitchen. No one in the garden, looking after the toads.

"Everyone said they would come if I rang the bell," Max told his dragon's egg.

It lay as silent as a stone.

"But would they?" asked Max. "If I rang it right now, would they come? They might say, 'He was all right five minutes ago. He can't be in trouble so soon!'"

"I bet they wouldn't come," said Max. "That's what I think. Maybe they wouldn't even hear it."

Max thought that there was nothing to do but ring the bell to find out. He rang it and rang it.

It boomed over the fields to the village, where the last of the crowd had just arrived home. They heard it, and they remembered their promise. They turned and rushed back the way they had come.

Max was so glad to see them that he made a small speech.

"Thank you," he said. "I was just testing to make sure you could hear it."

The crowd clapped. They were pleased to be thanked. They said it was a good idea to test the bell. Then they said goodbye, very kindly, and went home.

Max went back to see if his dragon's egg had hatched, and it hadn't.

"They all came!" said Max to the egg. "Everyone! Well, everyone, but Timmy."

Max gave a sigh. It would have been very nice if Timmy had come. "He was probably reading and didn't hear," said Max to the egg. "Sometimes he doesn't. I've noticed that."

The silence was awful.

"I bet no one would come if I rang that bell again!" Max said suddenly. They'd say, 'He's just testing,' and stay where they were!"

"That's what I think," said Max gloomily to the egg.

Max was wrong. They did come. Not as many this time, but still a crowd.

Max made another speech.

"I didn't think you'd come twice!" he said. "That's why I rang the bell! But you did. So thank you. Again."

No one clapped. They went home very soon, and they didn't wave goodbye.

"Timmy didn't come," said Max, back upstairs with his dragon's egg. "He must still be reading. They were cross," Max told the dragon's egg. "I should have said, 'Sorry' but I forgot. I'll ring the bell and say it now." So he did.

The people who came back looked very tired and very grumpy. They said, "We suppose you think this is funny! But we do not."

And then they went away.

Max went back up to his bedroom and he was so bored he almost thought he would tidy it up.

"I'm in trouble now," he told the egg. "No one's going to come now. Not even if I ring the bell till it cracks! Think of it! Me ringing the bell and ringing the bell, all by myself, and in terrible danger and no one coming to help ..."

This was such a sad idea that Max could hardly bear it. Sadly he went downstairs. Sadly he looked at the bell rope. Sadly he rang the bell, knowing no help would ever arrive.

Three people came.

Max was so happy to see them that he laughed out loud. No one else laughed, not even when he shouted, "I really didn't think anyone would come this time!"

They said, "Would you believe it?"

One of them was the old lady from the Children's Home.

"Max," she said. "Go and get your night things! We're taking you back with us. You can share Timmy's room."

For one moment Max thought that was a good idea. Then he thought of his dragon's egg. He couldn't possibly take it with him. It was much too heavy to carry so far. Anyway, no pets were allowed at the Children's Home. Not even rabbits. Most of all not baby dragons.

So Max did the only thing he could think of. He dashed inside and slammed the door. He thought they might come after him, but they didn't try at all. They gave up without any chase. He saw them through a window, trailing back across the evening fields. They looked so tired that he wanted to ring the bell and bring them back to say, "I'm sorry if you're tired because of me."

But he didn't.

Meanwhile, Timmy Green had been reading all day in his little bedroom in the Children's Home.

Timmy was frightened.

Every time the bell had rung Timmy was more frightened. He thought of toads and spiders and haunted attics. He thought about the dangerous dragon's egg that Max kept under his bed. And how Max didn't know how dangerous the egg was. But when the bell rang he couldn't make himself rush to the rescue when everyone else was rushing.

"There are plenty of people without me," he said to himself each time the bell rang, but he didn't feel good.

"I'm a coward," he told himself, "and I don't deserve a brave friend like Max.

Chapter 6
Dragon!

While Timmy was thinking about Max, Max was thinking about Timmy.

"What was it ..." he said, as he plodded up to his bedroom. "What was it that Timmy wanted to tell me about dragons' eggs. He said that they were dangerous! How can an egg be dangerous?"

Dragons, he knew, were quite safe. He had asked Aunt Emma about them once, soon after he found the egg.

"Dragons?" she had said, "Dangerous? Not if you know how to handle them! Messy? Yes. Dangerous? No. Rather like children."

Max opened his bedroom door. The dragon egg was still there, just as he had left it.

"Doesn't look dangerous to me!" said Max.

BANG!!!

Max fell over backwards so hard his head cracked against the wall. There was a smell like a million hard-boiled eggs. Chunks of shell as sharp and thick as broken flowerpots whizzed through the air. They hit the walls and made dents. They hit the ceiling and made dust fall in showers like dirty snow. One bit of shell thumped into the wooden door just behind Max and stuck there quivering like a knife.

At last Max knew what Timmy had been trying to tell him about dragons' eggs.

Dragons' eggs didn't hatch.

Dragons' eggs exploded!

"Gosh!" Max groaned and dragged himself to his feet. "I see why Timmy said they were dangerous!"

Max rubbed the dust from his eyes and remembered his problems had only just begun. There should be a dragon! Where was it? It was curled under his table, in the middle of a thick green puddle.

Sticky all over with a sort of eggy goo.

It smelled awful.

Max held out his hand and the dragon hissed and snarled. The size of the green puddle suddenly got bigger.

Anyone who knew anything about dragons, Aunt Emma, for instance, or Timmy Green, would have said, "What a beauty!" They would have seen its green and golden scales, its ruby eyes, and red shoulder ridges that would one day be wings. They would have known they were looking at something very, very special.

But it looked like a monster to Max.

And it smelled like a monster.

And it ate like a monster.

It ate a sock. It gulped it down as if it were starving. A pair of toads from the garden had followed Max upstairs. The dragon licked up one of them and turned towards the other.

"Stop!" shouted Max. He jumped to try and save the toad, slipped in the green goo, and cut his hand on a bit of eggshell.

The dragon swallowed up the toad, slid forward towards Max and licked up the blood on his hand. Then it tried to eat a wooden model of a Viking ship that had lain for several months under Max's table.

The ship did not go down as easily as socks and blood and toad. It had a sharp wooden mast that got stuck. The dragon croaked and choked and hissed. Max ran after it. He thumped the dragon's back when he could get near till the ship came up again, along with the sock and the toads, all of them in bits and pieces.

"I'm taking you outside!" Max told the dragon as it made another green puddle on the floor. "Not into the garden, you'll eat the toads. It will have to be the roof. I don't care what Timmy said about not keeping dragons on the roof!"

It wasn't easy to get the dragon on the roof. Max put a belt round the dragon's neck and tied some socks together to make a lead to pull the dragon along.

Out in the open air the baby dragon became more quiet. But it licked the blood from Max's cut hand in such a hungry kind of way that Max began to worry. He tied the sock-lead to a drainpipe, and thought about what he could feed the dragon.

"Sandwiches!" he remembered suddenly. "There are loads of sandwiches in the garden. I'll go and get some."

Chapter 7
Max in Trouble

The long summer day was coming to an end. In the village everyone but Timmy Green was very tired. They went to bed cross and early.

Max was also tired but there was no way he could go to bed. He had a dragon on the roof who needed supper.

Max pushed open the front door, and stepped out into the garden to collect the sandwiches. It was nice to breathe the fresh, undragonny air outside. He looked towards the village, where one light was shining. He looked up at the sky and saw the first star.

His witchy Aunt Emma always made him wish on the first star. She had told him the spell:

"Starlight, star bright,
First star I see at night,
Wish I may, wish I might,
Have the wish I wish tonight."

"I wish she would come back," said Max in a tired voice. "I wish Timmy was here. I wish the dragon would learn to be good. I wish everything would be all right in the morning."

More stars were coming out all the time. They shone like tiny sparks of silver. The pointed roofs looked sharp and black and high against the evening sky.

Just then Max heard something. A scrabbling sound, high up on the roof.

The sound grew louder. A head with two ruby eyes rose up, dark against the stars. There was the screech of claws on tiles. There was a frightened yowl.

Something slid down the roof and landed at Max's feet. It was part of the sock-lead.

Timmy had been right again.

You couldn't keep a dragon on a roof.

Max's dragon was halfway over the top already.

"Don't move till I get there!" yelled Max, and he flung down the sandwiches and ran. The bell rope tripped him up as he rushed through the door. DONG went the bell, just once.

Max didn't even notice.

He fled up all the dozens of stairs to the top of the house, went out onto the roof, across the flat place in the middle, and up the slope of the highest pointed roof.

He was just in time to catch the dragon's tail as it tumbled over the edge of the roof.

In the village Timmy was the only person who heard the bell ring. He put down his book and tip-toed outside. It was nearly dark, and very still.

Bang, bang, bang went Timmy's heart, thinking of toads and witches and ghosts and dragons.

He did not know what to do.

"If it rings again," he said at last, "I will wake someone up."

But it did not ring again. No one woke up. There was just Timmy, alone in the street. It was so quiet he began to hope he had dreamed the ringing of the bell.

But he knew that was not true and after a few more moments, he set off down the road.

"I had better be brave," said Timmy to Timmy. "Because there is only me."

Chapter 8
Timmy to the Rescue

Up on the roof Max and the dragon were not having a good time. The dragon and the top half of Max hung down on one side of the pointed roof that the dragon had climbed. The bottom half of Max hung down the other.

They were not very well balanced. Sometimes Max pulled the dragon a little bit backwards. Sometimes the dragon slipped and pulled them both a little bit forwards.

These were the worst times.

Max tried to think what to do. He had two choices. He could let go, or he could hold on.

He held on. He planned to hold on all night if he had to, and all the next day too, if he must.

After a while the dragon went to sleep, upside down, like a bat. Max became very cold and very, very bored.

"How odd," said Max, talking out loud to make the night seem less lonely, "How odd to be bored when you're hanging upside down in the dark, high up on a pointed roof and holding on to a dragon by the tail! And all alone because your witchy Aunt has vanished on her broomstick with a flash like lightning and a bang like a thunder storm! How can all that be boring?" Max asked himself.

"I don't know," said Max to Max, "but it is."

Meanwhile, Timmy was having a horrible walk. Every minute it had grown darker, every minute he had grown more scared. Now at last he was at the garden gate.

The first Max knew of this was an odd singing from far below him.

"Toads, toads, move out of the way!" Max heard.

"Toads, move out of the way! Please, toads! Because I can't see where you are in the dark! Toads."

Timmy, who was terribly afraid he'd step on a toad, was making his way to the front door.

A minute later he was knocking on it. Next, he was pushing it open, and calling out in a scared voice into the dark rooms, "Max! Max!" Then he was climbing the stairs.

Timmy found the two rooms at the top of the stairs. First he found Aunt Emma's room, as tidy as a picture in a book. Then he found the wild mess of a room that was where Max lived. He saw at once that the dragon's egg had hatched and it made his heart thump harder than ever.

He wanted to run away, but he didn't.
Instead he climbed the next lot of stairs. He
passed the attics that Max said were
haunted. He came out onto the roof, the high
flat place between the pointed roofs.

It was so dark that at first he couldn't see
Max, but he could hear him somewhere. A
squeaky voice said, "Help, help!" in an
uncomfy upside-down way.

"Where are you?" Timmy shouted, but then he saw the bottom half of Max hung over the highest peak. Timmy guessed the top half was not far away.

A moment later Timmy was scrabbling up the tiles to get hold of Max's ankles. In a minute he had got them and he pulled as hard as he could. Very soon after that Max toppled down on top of him. The baby dragon (still fast asleep) toppled down afterwards, and squashed them both.

"Thanks, Timmy," said Max. "I was getting really bored."

Chapter 9
Tidying Up

Now Max and Timmy had to decide what to do with the dragon. The easiest thing, since it was still asleep, was to put it to bed.

"But not in my room!" said Max.

So he and Timmy put the baby dragon to sleep in Aunt Emma's bed. It looked very comfy, tucked up under her black starry quilt.

"It's a very rare sort of dragon," whispered Timmy. "It may be the only one in the country."

"Good!" said Max. "One dragon like this is plenty! Have you seen what it's done to my bedroom? I don't think I'll ever be able to tidy it up."

"I don't think you'll ever be able to not tidy it," said Timmy.

So they tidied Max's bedroom. They flung the chunks of golden eggshell out of the window, mopped up the green puddles and swept away the dust. They shoved and rammed everything into drawers and cupboards and rubbish bins – all the clothes, bits of paper, apple cores, sticks, half-finished models, pencils, chalks, odd-shaped stones, empty mugs, tangled kites, dirty bottles and boots and shoes. They tidied all the things Max had collected over the last ten years.

It took them until two o'clock in the morning.

Then Max and Timmy took the blankets and pillows up onto the flat place on the roof and made their beds there. They couldn't sleep in Max's room because it still smelled very badly of hatching dragons. But it was tidy at last.

"Aunt Emma will be glad when she comes back and sees it," said Max.

"Max," said Timmy kindly, "I'm afraid people who have been struck by lightning don't normally come back."

"Oh," said Max with a yawn. "She wasn't struck by lightning. She went off on her broomstick to visit her friends at the edge of the world. She said she'd come back when I tidied my room."

"And I have," said Max, and fell asleep.

Chapter 10
Coming Home

When Max and Timmy woke up it seemed that the whole world had changed. Bright sunshine was shining down on their faces. They could hear a witchy voice.

"Down!" ordered the voice. "Sit! Sit! Good boy! Now, come!"

"She's back!" Max shouted. He had missed his witchy aunt very much, and he and Timmy flung off their blankets and rushed to climb the peak of the roof so that they could look down into the garden.

Black starry sheets and pillowcases were flapping on the washing line there. A small black figure and a green and golden one were working hard on the grass.

"Stay!" ordered Aunt Emma when she saw the boys looking, and the dragon stayed as still as a stone.

"It's a very rare one!" Timmy shouted down to her. "I've seen them in a book!"

"I've wanted one for years," Aunt Emma shouted back. "Hello Max!"

"Hello!" called Max, as happy as anything.

"I'm very glad to see you have tidied your bedroom at last, but next time you boys put a newly hatched baby dragon in my bed, please wash it first! And why are there sandwiches all over the lawn?"

"They came from the village," Max told her. "They brought them for me because they thought you'd been struck by lightning."

"Struck by lightning?"

"They don't believe you're a witch. No one ever does, do they, Timmy?"

"They think you're a nice old lady," said Timmy. "They don't think you're a witch, because you don't do spells."

"I do them all the time," said Aunt Emma, a bit crossly, and she fed the dragon a sandwich.

"I did one last night too," Max told her.

"Which one?"

"The star one."

"Did it work?"

"Yes," said Max, and he thought about his wishes. "Yes. It did."

That morning was the start of lots of good times. Max and Aunt Emma made friends again. The dragon grew more and more beautiful. Timmy came to Witches Towers for the longest sleepover ever (it lasted until he grew up).

Every day Timmy and Max walked across the fields together to Sleepy Hollow School. And one day the dragon went too. He tracked Max and Timmy all the way from Witches Towers.

The dragon was much bigger now. He was learning to fly, and he could already blow smoke that was almost hot.

The playground was suddenly empty – as if by magic.

Behind the dragon came Aunt Emma with her broomstick. Sparks flew out of her hair as she rushed to catch him.

"Stamp those sparks out!" shouted Timmy to the rest of the school, as he and Max ran to help her. "Stamp them out, or they'll scorch the grass!"

But no one came to help. Only when Aunt Emma had swept the dragon out of the playground with her broomstick did some of the children and teachers come out – very slowly. Then everyone stamped on the grass in a nervous way and said, "It's all right for you two! You're not scared because you're used to dragons and witches!"

This made Max and Timmy laugh very much.

"How do you know she's not just a nice old lady?" asked Max.

"Oh yes!" said everyone. "Whatever! Like we're going to believe that! Not!"

And when Max and Timmy heard this they laughed and laughed. They nearly fell over, laughing.

Barrington Stoke would like to thank all its readers for commenting on the manuscript before publication and in particular:

Robbie Bell
Kim Campbell
Amelia Davies-Green
George Day
Eleanor de Rohan
Kelly Evans
Daryl Leddy
Eleanor Lewis
Calum MacLean
Iona Moyle
Eliza Nenadich
Lily Perrett
Leah Peters
Harry Phillips
Isobel Robb
James Scott
Joy Thurman
Lily Walden
Lily Walters
Claire Welsh

Become a Consultant!

Would you like to give us feedback on our titles before they are published? Contact us at the email address below – we'd love to hear from you!

info@barringtonstoke.co.uk
www.barringtonstoke.co.uk

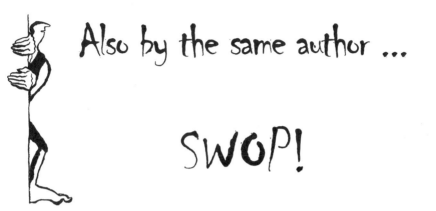

Also by the same author ...

SWOP!

Tom and Emily live with wicked Aunty Bess, the worst aunt in the world. They don't have proper beds. The food is so bad, they *like* their school dinners. And they even have to cut her extra long toenails!

Lucky for them, Emily's good at swops! She swops their gran for a donkey – but can she swop their horrid home for a happy ending?

More exciting new titles ...

Enna Hittims
by
Diana Wynne Jones

Anne Smith is sick of being sick. So she makes up stories about Enna Hittims – a brave hero, as big as Anne's finger, with a magic sword that cuts anything. It's the best game ever ... until Enna comes to life!

You can order *Enna Hittims* directly from our website at **www.barringtonstoke.co.uk**

King John

and the Abbot

by

Jan Mark

King John – Rich but greedy. He has all of England.

The Abbot – Rich but rude. He has a problem.

The Shepherd – Poor, but clever. He has nothing at all (except a scruffy dog).

King John has given the Abbot 3 puzzles. If the Abbot gets them wrong, King John will cut off his head! Can Jack save the Abbot's neck?

You can order *King John and the Abbot* directly from our website at: **www.barringtonstoke.co.uk**